Bachelor Auction Boss

Alex Ankarr

Published by Alex Ankarr, 2015.

This is a work of fiction. Similarities to real people, places, or events are entirely coincidental.

BACHELOR AUCTION BOSS

First edition. February 7, 2015.

Copyright © 2015 Alex Ankarr.

Written by Alex Ankarr.

2nd edition published 05/05/2015: previously published as 'Sold As A Slave.'

Bachelor Auction Boss

"WHAT'LL YOU BID ME for this exceptionally attractive specimen, then, ladies and gentlemen? Handsome creature, isn't he? Brawny, obviously spent a fair bit of time in the gym, a six-footer I think..." And here, the auctioneer leans in to Will and scrutinizes the top of his head, seeing if he can judge Will's height, and squaring up to him as if to compare it to his own. (Which is around five feet nine or ten, so Will is actually pretty insulted by the imputation that he may not actually scrape the six foot mark. He does, he certainly does, just for the record, if anyone wants to know. Quite comfortably, in fact. Six foot *one*, actually. Not that he's a bit sensitive about it, coming from a family of near-giants and being the shrimp of the clan, or anything. Ho-hum. No not at all.)

"Yes, definitely a six-footer," the auctioneer announces. Brewster, is it? Will's pretty sure the guy's name is Brewster. Like there was any doubt! Will's beginning to feel his temper shorten, get ragged at the edges, and he's not feeling too comfortable either. Not psychologically – what with all the potential buyers crowding around the auction block, peering and leering at him and turning to one another to discuss his attractions and uses. It's a startling experience.

And he's not physically at ease, either. The manacles are nipping, cold and heavy, at his wrists and his ankles, and the chains only add to the weight and the bulk. And the toga they put him in, before the sale? Aren't togas supposed to cover more of the body than, well, *this*? Aren't they supposed to cover your ass, for a start? Well, you could say that this one does, perhaps. Just about, and only with the aid of regular, periodic tugging at the hanging fabric to the rear – his rear – from Will himself. Still he's overly conscious that it's all a question of angle and viewpoint, as to what kind of a view the assembled potential clientèle might get, if they peer and crook their necks and crane to get a really good look.

Which some of them certainly appear to be doing, and it's a real battle to keep an eye on them. To keep turning and twisting his torso around – dragging his literal ball and chains with him as he goes – to prevent them getting an eyeful of his ass. And that's even if his ass is the only thing they get a view of. It's not as if he was allowed any underwear before he got himself up on this podium, to be sold off as if he was a chattel or a nice bit of livestock, to the highest, hungriest bidder.

God, it's humiliating. And the only thing that enables Will to treat the whole experience with any kind of equanimity, any degree of *savoir-faire* and assurance, is the face that's gazing at him, right from the back of the auction room. It's the face of his assistant, Jon. And it's looking right at his own face, not his ass or, well, anything else. It's not craning, it's not straining for a better view of what's for sale.

His assistant, yeah. Because this is a charity bachelor auction, set up by the human resources department of the industrial engineering company where he's a senior director. Well, what other conclusion would anyone come to? That they're in an ancient Roman amphitheatre and any moment now the Christians and the lions are about to come roaring out of the opened portcullis, tearing each other to pieces?

No. Will is a volunteer, here. Even if a slightly reluctant, emotionally black-mailed one. (The charity involved is for an illness that the assistant head of the human resources department's daughter suffers from, and she is accordingly evangelical and ruthless in her conscription of one and all for any charitable ef-forts on its behalf. Basically there's *no escape*, not when Elizabeth takes it into her head to volunteer you, and the event hall gets booked. Will accepted his fate two weeks back, when Liz informed him – much more than asked him – about his role, the date picked and the outfit he'd be wearing. Well, after a few protests about *community consensus*, and *modelling behaviors*, and *sexual harassment*, and *completely inappropriate costumes...* (Will was holding out for a tux and bow-tie. He still can't understand how a tux and bow-tie wouldn't have been awesome. He looks *totally badass and secret-agent on a mission* in a tux. It should be on his resume. 'Can rock a tux like nobody's business.') And how he'd much rather just whip out his wallet and make a less effortful and public donation. Liz had steam-rollered, countered and quashed all of his protests, established a commu-nity-wide platform of popular support and dragged him kicking and screaming into her latest master-plan. And he gave in, accepted it.

Partly, he accepted it because there was a bright side to the news. (However dire it might be.) Because, well, in a charity auction, you never know who's going to bid for you, who's going to win your company for the night. (Or who's going to win your body and your services, even if for a *strictly time-limited* five hours until the evening is over, or when the purchaser decides that a disastrous date is over, whichever is earliest. But all of it on the strictest understanding that successful purchase, within the terms of this event, is to be taken to mean, basically, a date with added embarrassment for the datee, as a result of their outfit and BDSM gear. No guaranteed getting lucky at the end of the night, for the lucky purchaser.

This, to Will, seems like a bad dream, and he intends to treat it as one once he's successfully auctioned off. Have a few drinks – with kind permission of his lucky winner – get a little merry, dance a dutiful once or twice (with his ball and chain temporarily removed) and go home thankfully at the end of the night. Feeling that he's done his duty by the company and the charity thoroughly, and only mildly dreading whatever scheme or dream Liz might spring up out of her twisted brain next time.

Unless... unless Jon bids on him. That might be a different experience. Well, an altogether pleasanter experience. Not that he's relying on it. Why would Jon want to buy his company for the night? He almost certainly gets more than enough of it on a daily basis, fulfilling Will's every request and requirement with ruthless efficiency, delegating the minor errands to the couple of interns he's taken on and inducted and trained perfectly, keeping Will's calendar running like clockwork, updating his own skills and industry know-how like a machine-precise, thoroughly-oiled dream. And generally being very *distracting*.

Generally being rather beautiful, in a soft-eyed mild-mannered way, that doesn't accord at all with his tough-minded ruthlessness with suppliers and contractors, his careful, encyclopedia-informed implacability when he's assisting Will in deal negotiations. Being quietly funny and dryly charming in private conversation. Not seeming to take Will all that seriously, and yet making his professional life easy and satisfying and pleasant in all the ways it can be. Making him feel comfortable, secure, knowing that someone has his back, knowing that someone is looking out for his interests, that he comes *first* for Jon.

He probably does, on a professional level. Undoubtedly. Jon reports directly to him. But it's a little dangerous to be feeling that way, because the feeling is undoubtedly less than professional. It doesn't just feel like a professional thing. And he shouldn't be allowing himself to feel that way. He only hired Jon less than five months ago. The way he's feeling is getting to seem ridiculous.

It's not as if Jon is going to bid on him *anyway*. The *idea* is ridiculous.

"Ladies and gentlemen, we are about to get the bidding underway. What do you offer me, for this handsome specimen, this exceptionally well-muscled bit of beefcake? Check out that rear-end, ladies, those are some nice glutes. And I can tell that one or two of you have been appreciating them already, maybe before today even. Oh, don't think I can't tell, you hens, you're shocking! Are you blushing, madam, yes, the red-head in the corner!?" Jon doesn't turn to look to see who he's talking to. He's too busy blushing himself. God, this is *excruciating*. What if he doesn't even get a bid? That would be humiliating.

"First bid of the night, ladies and gentlemen! Do I hear a hundred dollars? Minimum bid, please note to all assembled interested parties, one hundred dollars!"

There's an indistinct cry – from the corner of the event room the auction is being held in – and it's more of a squawk, really. And from Will's peripheral vision, he catches a glimpse of an upraised arm to accompany the high-pitched squawk. "One hundred dollars!" the auctioneer booms, clearly pleased with the starting bid. "Thank you, madam! Will anyone give me one hundred twenty?"

And oh God. Will is pretty sure – red-head, screechy voice, a taste for green overwrought highly-diamanté'd evening dresses? That has to be Carol, senior advisor in the accounts department. Not his type, although she's been giving him the eye and dropping heavy clodhopping hints for a good six months now. God, not his type *at all*.

Jon is his type. If he was forced to admit it. And has been from the first time Will set eyes on him, strolling out from his second interview onto the short-list and smiling at the receptionist, sleeves of his cheap interview suit rucked up and his hands in his pockets. He hadn't even noticed Will, out at the edges of the lobby as he waited for the elevator. Will hadn't bothered to conduct the interviews himself. It was only for a fixed-term assistant, and he goes through those like a knife through butter. None of them last long.

Jon has lasted six months now, and that's a record. Of course the short-list was something that Will made short work of, once he'd copped a good look at Jon. What short-list? There was no short-list. Jon was the only possible candidate. Well, as far as Will was concerned, anyhow, and his was the only opinion that mattered, on the subject of his own assistant.

And now Will is being auctioned off – for the evening – or a few hours of his time are being hired out, at any rate – to any one of a couple of thousand prospective 'dates', including Jon. Of course Jon is here. As an employee of the company, as Will's assistant, as the helpful person who put in a few hours in HR, without having to, researching a venue and guest-list and caterers for Elizabeth's baby, the main event on the company's social calendar for the next few months. And as a guest, of course – all done up in tux and black tie, and so handsome in them that it makes Will's heart ache with a sour sore twitch, although he covers it well whenever Jon's around. It wouldn't be fair to put him on the spot, to make it clear that his direct boss has a terrible aching crush on him.

It's not just his heart that aches, either. Although he'd better keep that under control, in this flimsy little toga, Will thinks. A whole lot of deep, deep embarrassment could ensue, otherwise.

Jon's a guest, just the same as all the other guests here tonight. All of them paying ridiculous ticket prices out of deep pockets – well, the clients, anyway – for the benefit of Liz's charity. And ready to bid more of the readies for a bit of fun and a bought-and-paid-for companion for the night – who they might otherwise know as a friend and colleague. Or boss.

Because Jon could perfectly well bid for Will tonight, for his company and his 'services' and his time, even just for an evening. And if only he *would*, Will thinks, and it's embarrassing just how deeply he means it, how heartfelt his hopeless wishing is. He could break his own heart with the depth of that wishing, with the yearning he feels whenever he looks up from his own screen or phone in his executive office and sees Jon bending his head over his phone, sending a text to a supplier or detailing meeting room requirements or discussing new packaging legalities with one of the warehouse guys.

Jon always seems to catch him at it, always looks up and smiles at just the crucial moment. And Will always flushes, looks down quickly, wonders if Jon suspects. He's a sweet guy, though. He's not going to hold it against Will, or mock him for it. Will tries not to wonder whom he goes home to, if anyone. He never asks those kinds of questions. Better not to know.

"One hundred twenty, thank you sir, that's one hundred twenty. I'm looking around the room and asking for one thirty, yes madam. Now, that's all very well, ladies and gents, but a bit stingy for this fine specimen of manhood before you. Take a look at the heft and sinew on those arms, those shoulders, sir! Good strong thighs, nice rear end, pretty hair and eyes if you have a fancy for that sort of thing…"

Christ, the bastard is waxing lyrical, Will thinks, alarmed. If he didn't know better he might speculate that this guy is after Will's ass himself. If he hadn't already spotted him in the reception room, getting over-familiar with someone else's attractive blonde wife, and very narrowly escaping a cornering and a stiff word – if not a battering – outside in the parking lot. Maybe he's just had a couple of drinks prior to getting up on the auction block?

But he's certainly giving it everything he's got, you have to give the freak that much. "How about one hundred and fifty, gentlepeople, commercial interests, bystanders and layabouts? Come on, loosen up your pockets, guys, remember it's for charity! Let me hear one hundred and fifty, people! Come on, he's all yours for the night, do with him as you wish, get a load of those glutes, people! I know you're having some dirty thoughts about this fine hunk of rump-steak and his rump!"

Will is blushing excruciatingly at this point, because who wouldn't? And worse than this – possibly effective, who knows – sales spiel being directed at him and his supposed charms, is the audience it's being sold to. Which contains Jon, oh *God*. Not that he'll care. Not that he'll even be listening, probably. (God, Will hopes that he isn't listening.) He's probably in a corner chatting up some pretty young thing, never giving a thought to his poor boss being embarrassed up on the stage in the name of a good cause. Which is probably better. It isn't as if Jon would dream of bidding on him. As Will has told himself approximately a million times and seventeen, now.

"Okay, one fifty." It's called out fairly softly from a corner of the hall, and Will knows the voice, too. He *knows* the voice.

And he cranes his head around just the same, jerking around quickly. He must look a real sight in this get-up and with his legs and arms on show, and very nearly his ass and other parts too. And looking around like a fluffy fragile chick that's lost its henny mom. He can't see for a moment. But then he sees an arm lifted, that drops as he looks.

It's Jon. And yeah, it's Jon who's just bid for him. Christ, it's crazy the jolt of adrenalin *that* sends through his chest. And only more so when Jon turns his head, and actually catches Will's eye. He smiles slightly. And then dips his head down. Is that a pinkening of his cheeks, Will thinks, is it really? Is Jon blushing? He doesn't think he's ever seen Jon blush. He's normally the epitome of calm, as unflappable as you can possibly imagine, cool and organised and keeping Will's professional life running just like it's on rails.

And secretly, furtively, Will dreams about destroying that unflappable calm of Will's. Destroying it in extremely specific ways. Ones that involve country hotel weekends and breakfast in bed and probably, why not go the whole clichéd hog, champagne and rose petals somewhere along the line. Kisses that go everywhere, straying into places to make Jon flush and sweat and moan... Not that he would ever say so. He's so embarrassingly shy with the guy that he probably comes over as intimidatingly uptight. No doubt Jon jokes about his tight-ass boss with his co-workers, while Will is busy day-dreaming about Jon's ass...

And Will has to get his head back in this game and pay some attention to the course of events. Because it's not like the auctioneer's brought down the gavel on Jon's bid, and handed him off to his assistant, announced that he's done for the day and gone home. Although Will wishes that he would. Devoutly, he wishes that he would.

"I have one hundred and fifty bid, ladies and gentlemen and the rest of you rabble," the auctioneer announces triumphantly. "To the young gentleman in the natty suit over by the French windows, that's the one, thank you, sir!" And he indicates Jon with a flourish that's clearly intended to maximise his embarrassment, since that's half the fun for everyone on charity nights like this one.

And he doesn't look up, doesn't face the guy or Will himself out with any of his usual trademarked chill composure. No, instead he ducks his head down and doesn't meet a single eye. He's shy as a schoolboy suddenly, and it couldn't be less like Jon. Will almost feels for him over it, sympathises. Then he recollects that *he's* the one who's barely dressed – barely decent, in fact – and set up in front of a baying crowd of slightly inebriated and highly hormonal women, being hooted at. And he's already had a few really indecent propositions made to him. And the manacles and chains are genuine, not plastic, and rubbing him raw. Also the gladiator sandals, while probably flattering to his calves as a mid-distance runner, are uncomfortable. Liz definitely has some kind of gladiator-fetish going on. Will would sooner face the lions than these ladies, though.

And more than half of these people are a little bit drunk, or a bit more than that, and all of them are colleagues to Will, or subordinates, or business contacts. That's fine right now, because he's not really focused on them. He's totally focused on Jon. No, on the auction itself, he corrects quickly. But later on, it's not like they're going to forget tonight in a hurry, and he has more than a feeling that this is going to take a lot of living down. What happens at this charity auction, is not just going to stay at this charity auction. Pictures from tonight are practically certain to wind up all over social media, and Will can't help but flinch whenever someone openly lifts their phone up, when a flash startles him.

None of it matters, though. Not compared to Jon having expressed some... polite interest, in taking on Will as a companion for the evening, a little fetching eye-candy on his arm for the night. Is it just polite, though? Will's heart sinks at the thought, because what if this is just an employee bidding up the price for his boss, as a matter of flattery and adroit career enhancement? Because he doesn't want Will's temper soured by going for a bargain-bin hundred bucks, because it wouldn't look good for the department? Because it's for charity after all, and Jon's a nice guy?

"One seventy!" comes a screech from close by the stage, close enough to be loud even without amplification, and Will searches about for the culprit, the source. Hell, and the news couldn't be much worse. It's one of the gaggle of hen-night types from Marketing, a little unsteady on her heels and fighting to get as close to the stage as she can, grinning at her whooping pals when she isn't leering at Will. (She's leered at Will before now, at Marketing strategy meetings and company bonding exercises, and he's barely managed to avoid her attentions with some sharp moves and a lot of extremely adroit handling. God knows what an evening spent at her beck and call, under her command would be like. He doesn't want to consider it.)

"One ninety!" And before Will can even begin to put in a few prayers, to urge the gods and the fates to be merciful, and allow him to escape such a fate as being forcible datee to that unconscionable harpy would entail, there's a further bid in. From almost anyone it would be welcome in comparison, although he doesn't even make the ghost of an attempt to kid himself. A second competing bid from Jon is what he's really hoping for, and his head jerks in the direction of the cry.

He catches Jon's eye, because yes, it's from the right quarter of the room, and he's just dropping his hand, and... yeah. It's him, and if Will breaks out into a silly sappy grin then he's barely got enough self-consciousness to care. Even when he's barely wearing a toga – a sheet with a few safety-pins, let's get real – and a little body-glitter. (Hey, the body-glitter was applied with his attention distracted, while being prepared by a couple of Elizabeth's assistants – or assassins – for his upcoming starring role. He was being argued into submission by Elizabeth, when he had a very last-chance revulsion and panic and tried to back out. Will has zero responsibility for the body glitter. He's not copping to that one.)

And Jon blushes. And that's a staggerer. Since when does Jon blush about *anything*, anytime anywhere? Never. Jon is possibly the least blush-prone, most self-possessed twenty-two year old that Will has ever encountered in his life. He has abnormal amounts of *savoir-faire* and tranquillity, is technically adept in four separate engineering disciplines, speaks a handful of languages to fluency and has never been visibly discomfited in any social situation, that Will has witnessed. He may conceivably be the most intimidatingly self-possessed young person that Will knows. (He may conceivably be a charmingly engineered automaton.) It may be part of what Will loves in him. (And that's an internal admission, even if there's only himself to hear it, that might have been better off never made. Sleepless nights and yearning and wistful fantasies, he's endured, these past few months, as uncomplainingly as he can manage it. But he's been able to minimise it thus far, calling it a fancy or a fixation or even a crush, to himself. Even infatuation lately, when it's been getting really bad. Like really, really, really hellish bad. But now he's gone and called it love, he's made it official to himself and how in the name of hell is he ever going to get over this now? How often in a person's life do they really truly fall in love?

Jon's almost ten years younger than him, but there's something about Jon that makes him feel taken care of, the younger party. And how long is it since he's felt that way about anyone he's dated? He's making too much money for that, has too much power at work, has lived long enough to gain an external composure and vibe of his own of sophistication and know-how. No-one would ever feel like they needed to take care of *Will*. No-one ever seems to, any more, anyhow. Except Jon. Who is very subtly pushy with him, sometimes, who tells him off in an only partially joking way, when he stays out late with friends and is slightly hungover in the morning. Who preps him for big-deal meetings and negotiations, to such a degree that Will's become the primary deal-maker and sales-dynamo for the company in the months since Jon started work with him. Seriously, Jon could be described as obsessional. Will has never previously received professional support on this level, not like since Jon began at the company.

He only wishes he really truly belonged to Jon, was dating him, and the very thought sends a vibrant hot shudder through him. And just as long as no-one

else places a bid, that fantasy can come true, at least for the space of an evening...
"Two hundred and fifty!"

Damn it. That sure as hell isn't Jon. As if he's going to bid against himself anyway. (Would Jon consider Will worth shelling out two hundred and fifty bucks of his own money? Doubtful. That he's even gone this far is a selfless act. If he actually winds up landed with Will for the evening, then Will will surely have to reimburse him for the expenditure. Possibly out of company funds, but it may as well come out of his own pocket. He owes Jon something, for sure, for the service way above and beyond the call of duty that he's been expending all of these months.)

Damn, the lights are bright. It's like they've been turned up in the past minute or so, purposely to prevent Will from deciphering just who is involved in the battle for his company for the next few hours. (And he's kidding, he's kidding, he's *totally kidding* on that one.) He can't make out who it is who's calling out confirmation, because the auctioneer apparently didn't catch the numbers involved and requires a repetition. Then, with his hand shading his eyes, he catches sight – because right in the middle of the crowd, there in the heart of it, is Greg from the art department. Is Greg the name? He barely knows the guy. And he's waving his arms like a crazy person, yelling, "Yeah! Yeah! Two fifty! Bargain!" at the auctioneer.

He's not even looking at Will. Will feels a little awkward on his behalf. Because Greg is normally a pretty cool guy. By reputation at least, since Will doesn't know him that well himself. But not right now. Most everyone here is a little addled from all of the free champagne on offer – hell, it's a charity function, after all. Get 'em a little sauced, fired up like a rocket, a firework, and relax their intuition and judgement. Give the guy in charge a little auction hammer and watch 'em go, bidding way more than they ever would sober, for things they'll wince to think about in six months' time! So everyone is – not loaded, but a little way along the road to loaded. But Greg, he's further along that road than anyone else is, it looks a lot like. He's flailing a little bit, he's gesticulating more than is conceivably really necessary, he's practically bellowing out his bid amount. And he's, yeah, swaying a little bit, on the balls of his feet. And leaning against a pillar – not casually for effect, either.

He's drunk enough to be flushed, and flushed enough to be hot, and hot enough to be scratching and pulling at the hem of his thin silk shirt. (Somewhere along the line he's discarded his suit jacket.) Hot in both senses, Greg is, your standard boho artist with a business-unfriendly personal style, hair noticeably too long for any other department, lashes thick, mouth sensual. (Yes, Will has noticed. He's hung up on Jon, but that doesn't mean he's lost the use of his eyes.) Pulling at the hem, he's revealing his navel, a trace of fine chest hair running down that far, the coy beginnings of a happy-trail. (Will's eyesight is excellent, actually, thank you.) And he's stretching up one arm to flex and straighten, close to yawning, which also gives a nice view of his biceps, and the depth of his chest.

Yeah, he's pretty, what's the big deal, move along now please folks. It's not that easy for Will to just automatically move along, though. Not considering that Greg is pretty – actually super-pretty, to be quite frank. And bidding more than a couple of hundred bucks for the privilege of an evening spent in the company of, well, Will. (In the company of Will dressed in a shortie toga, and locked up in a ball and chain, to be more specific. Will isn't going to split hairs here. Not even chest-hairs. (Although it does make him wonder a little about Greg's tastes.) Maybe the booze is a factor that's warping Greg's short-term judgement, maybe it's contributing to his decision here. But even so.

Will isn't above admitting that he's a little bit flattered.

And the auctioneer is in the middle of his clarification, and then done with it. And then making ready to bring the gavel down, with a throaty, gravelly rumble of, "Two hundred and fifty dollars! I'm bid two hundred and fifty here by this gentleman, ladies and gentlemen! Who's going to offer–"

But that's the full distance he gets, because he's shouted down, overruled, conquered by volume. "Three hundred," a sharp, incisive voice spits out, and then repeats it, "Three hundred," more quietly. It's still audible, over the chatter of the crowd. Which is dying down, because people around him, and close to the stage, and sprinkled further out, are beginning to be faintly aware that there's the beginnings of a drama being played out here. It's nascent, but swelling speedily, promising tears or blood spilt. Or a lot of money to a worthy cause, which wouldn't be quite equal the fun, but a bonus nonetheless.

But the hive awareness is fuzzy, congealed, not pin-sharp and brilliantly compelling like the clarity of Will's perception right now. It's Jon who made that last bid, the one that countermanded Greg's two-fifty. And this time he wasn't looking at Will as he called it out, and he isn't looking at him *now* as he pushes a little way forward in the crowd. (Because Will can see him through the bright haze of the lights. It's difficult, and it doesn't help with focus, and scanning a crowd speedily and accurately, but Will can do it. He'd be willing to bet that he will always be able to track down and identify Jon, no matter the depth and milling masses of the crowd. In pitch darkness. Even on an alien planet. Always, he would always be able to.

Maybe he's a little far gone. On love, it must be, because he's barely had a drop of the free champagne. And it's quite nice stuff, too.

Will could happily have the whole thing end right here, because this is an outcome that he could live with. Yeah, stop right here.

"Four hundred," Greg announces. He does so with his arm languidly waving in the air in the vague direction of the auctioneer, with the air of someone who believes that they've put the final kibosh on someone else's aspirations and pretensions. (Greg can, by reputation, be kind of an ass.) And Greg, too, is moving closer to the stage. And now he smiles directly up at Will, and yep, yep, there's no denying truthfully that Greg is attractive. Pity he knows it so very well. His eyes travel up and down Will's body, like he's assessing which part he'd most like to begin consuming. Will is actually marginally senior to Greg within the company, technically. He resists the urge to step forward to the lip of the stage, kneel down and remind the asshole of this inconvenient fact.

Partly, he refrains from doing it because of the length of his toga. And, for reasons she claimed had to do with the 'line' and 'fall' of the fabric, Elizabeth has ferociously barred him from wearing briefs or shorts underneath. He's feeling a little unsecured and vulnerable, here.

Partly he refrains, because Greg isn't honestly that important, here. The auctioneer is announcing, "Four hundred, guys! Four hundred dollars I'm offered! Anyone here want to go one better than four hundred? Come on, people! This is a very worthy cause we're talking about!" But Will isn't looking at the auctioneer, and he's not looking at Greg, pretty as he is.

Because Jon's still getting closer – pushing through the crowd, not aggressive but pretty assertive, and definite enough that anyone who isn't initially paying attention, too enthralled by the on-stage spectacle, quickly gets the general idea. He catches Will's eye as he comes closer, and oh, he's not smiling any more. "Six," he snaps, with a quick snap of the head towards the auctioneer. Who's getting a little too close to just looking befuddled. It's like he's starting to get the feeling there's actually some sort of drama going on here, but hasn't quite worked out exactly what it might be yet.

Jon looks... purposeful, now. He's got just that no-prisoners-no-mercy look he gets when he's getting Will up to speed on a real hardball business negotiation, making sure he's weaponned up to the jeweled hilt and has everything he needs to take down the competition, if he can't convert them to his way of thinking. That's the way he looks until the last moment, when he sends Will off into the lion's den, to face the opposition and bring back the bacon for the company. His face softens, usually, at that last moment. The last time, the last big deal, he'd clapped Will on the shoulder, moments before the last minute when he'd have to show his face. Then impulsively hugged him, fiercely tight like a ligature, a tourniquet around his chest.

Well, that had never happened before. It maybe shook Will out of his stride a little bit, and the same when Jon abruptly let go of him, and stepped back quick like Will was a hot thing off of a hot griddle and he'd burned his fingers. "Sorry," he'd said, and Will hadn't known exactly what to do with that comment, how to interpret it. What d'you say to that? *"It's fine, buddy, and how about another while we're at it, and if you wanted to grab my ass then that would also be a-okay, be fine with me?"* No. That probably – almost certainly – wouldn't have been appropriate. He'd smiled – tamping it down, keeping it small, not burning up with the light he'd felt inside. That's the only time, so far, that Jon's hugged him.

He's close and getting closer, in the midst of the buzzing and curious crowd, although he hasn't quite got as near as Greg yet. But Greg's heard, and Will can identify the moment, right there on his face, when he becomes aware of Jon, of Jon's onward progress towards the stage, of who his competitor in the gladiatorial combat of the auction room is. That there is a combat going on, even.

It's clear, too, the moment that his eyes meet Jon's. He's too, uh, relaxed and limber for his body to stiffen or his eyes to narrow. Relaxed, that's a synonym for drunk, right? Jon isn't drunk, though, and really Will only realises it right in that moment. Most everyone else in this auction room has taken at the least a drink or two or two and a half this evening. Jon doesn't usually drink much, but normally he'd have one drink and maybe two at a professional social function, just to be sociable, at least.

Will knows him pretty well, though. He knows, just knows, that Jon is stone cold sober. Stone cold sober, as he lifts his eyes and looks up at Will where he's standing, minimally clothed, up on stage in front of an ogling crowd. Jon smiles, slowly, as his eyes travel up from the sandals and their laces criss-crossing Will's calves, up his knees and the beginning of his thighs, from the hem of his toga and flickering sideways. They drift on, to the weight of Will's ball and chains (and HR have gone to amazing lengths regarding verisimilitude) and on upwards. (And Will pulls at the hem of his toga self-consciously, because, because, he doesn't really even know why.) To his chest, his arms (and Will is something of a gym obsessive) and then, his face.

It's... comprehensive. That look definitely covers everything. And Jon has never, never looked at him quite like that before. Will feels himself flush up underneath the weight of it. That look is *inappropriate*. He struggles to come up with any other word for it, but that's what springs to mind, and damned if he can come up with something else more suitable, less charged with disapproval instead. From a subordinate, an underling, to the guy he works for? How is that appropriate?

That's not the same thing as saying that he doesn't like it. It's amazing how he feels his cheeks scald, his lashes bat down to his cheeks under that fierce and speculative scrutiny. Do the things that that look suggests really go through Jon's mind when he looks at Will? Or is a toga and BDSM costume responsible for so much?

"I am bid six hundred dollars for this fine piece of... manflesh," the auctioneer says. And thank God, just thank God, that he didn't say 'ass', Will thinks. Although it wouldn't make all that much difference, because that's effectively what's going on here and everyone knows it too, whether anyone says it out loud or not. And God help him, because Jon is pushing closer to the stage, closer and closer. And Will has to wonder what kind of a view that affords him, where this damn toga is concerned. And his eyes, his eyes are brighter than the lights in here. They could illuminate the place by themselves. They could illuminate the sky, if the stars were doused. And Jon shouts out to the auctioneer – and to the crowd, because a low rumbling ululation has started up, a humming buzz that's quiet, quiet, less quiet, getting louder – and his shout is *this*. "Seven hundred and fifty. Seven fifty. *Mine.*"

You would think those words were from the lips of a crazy person. Isn't that something that a crazy person would do? "Ah, sir," the auctioneer points out – and he sounds cautious, and well he might, he's dealing with a crazy person, be careful, people! – "I should point out that you're bidding against yourself here. Am I to take that as a binding and intentional bid for the, ah, services and company of this gentleman for the remainder of the evening?"

Jon's eyes glint at Will. And although he speaks to the auctioneer, loud and clear, it's still Will that he's looking at, eyes locked. Jon has never been what anyone would call shy, not from day one of his employment, and he's not the sort to shy away from eye-contact. But this is different, his eyes have never locked on Will's and frankly challenged him this way before. "I said seven fifty," he repeats. Yeah, notionally to the auctioneer, that's right.

And the guy shrugs, because who is he to turn down a paying punter's money? Jon's greenbacks are just as good as anyone's, and if your card ain't rejected then you is perfectly welcome, sir. Even if you're friggin' bughouse nuts as an ants' nest in June. With baking soda poured over it.

And Will can't deny that he feels a frisson, a helix of fire looping around his spine at the tone of Jon's voice as he absently spits it out, more fierce and dismissive than Will's ever heard him. (And he's heard him be both, often.) That's the exact tone he heard in Will's voice in the first couple of months of his job with the company, back before Will's budding, pleasant fancy for his attractive new assistant had grown and matured, into something difficult and complex that was hurting his heart every day. Back then – well, that makes it sound an eon ago, when it's only a few scant months. But anyway – then, Will was still dating around a little, both girls and guys, still looking, still single, hoping for a solid connection but always open to some hot casual action too. Then, he'd been okay with Jon fielding his personal calls at work, as well as the business contact ones. Now, he'd be much more reticent about doing the same. Except that now, he's not mostly dating at all any more. No, too busy pining his ass off, for the assistant organising his life into a model of lethal efficiency and smooth running.

Jon, back then, dealt with any calls from dates or people Will had slept with, with... well... a curiously violent and abrupt kind of efficiency. You might almost call it terse. Or possibly cold. One way or another, a lot of first and second dates around that time had failed to lead on to anything more. And the odd one-night stand had proved to be just that, without Will doing anything to discourage such bed-partners, and indeed now and then having suggested a second bout of fun and hi-jinks. Walking in on Jon fielding such calls, remembering the tone of his voice then, renders the tone in it now jarringly familiar.

But he has other things to think on, now.

There's definitely increased audience participation at this point. There are cheers, jeers, growls and leers going on, and picking up in frequency and volume. Will's starting to feel like a cheap burlesque act, and he isn't impressed when the crazy Marketing girls press closer to the stage, including the lady of the early bid. They yell out raucous pleas for a better look at what's on sale. *On sale.* Christ. When one of them half-launches herself over the lip of the stage, to make a grab for his ankle, Will is quite ready to issue her a sharp reproof. Or shove her ass back off-stage. And thank God that that's going to be the highest the drunken harlot can reach, because being groped for a good cause is not what Will signed up for when Elizabeth talked him into this whole exercise in pandemonium. He's not a piece of *meat*, after all.

But he doesn't need to utter one word or take a step back, because evidently he has a white knight, if not on a steed then mobile and quick, leaping to his defence. Not Jon, unfortunately, which would be the most palatable option as far as Will is concerned. (Although, even then, hey, he's a grown man. And senior to an awful lot of people here. Including Jon himself. And...)

And Greg. Who's there, suddenly, instantaneously, pressed close to the stage as any of these shrieking harpies. Not laying a finger on any of 'em including Will's admirer – 'cause everybody's a gentleman, here, right? - but close enough to attract her attention. And he's sufficiently broodily looming to be at least a little intimidating, without putting his clear objections to her current behaviour into words. So that she turns her head, aware of the looming shadow cast over her – and the alerted and suddenly alarmed and inebriated expression on her sweaty runny-eyeliner'd face is, okay, pretty funny. She gives him a briefly considering look, and suddenly appears to remember that she really needs to dive back into the security of her girl posse and get the hell out of Dodge.

And not that it's not a relief, but Will is insulted by the implication that he needed *rescuing*. But an interjection wouldn't serve him any. Because Greg, swaying and propping himself up against the edge of the podium, is too busy swinging a pointy finger in the direction of the auctioneer, and announcing in slightly slurred words, "Eight fifty. I'm good for it, he's totally worth it, and I'm not giving up and going home until that gavel goes down on my winning bid, folks!"

This gets a ragged, giggling cheer. And the auctioneer seems to sag a bit, visibly leaning on the auction block, like he's not quite sure just how much more of this any poor gavel-wielder should be expected to take. "Eight fifty, then," he says into the mic, with a despairing and boggled expression. "Eight fifty, folks. Whaddya say? Anyone want to top that? Somebody?" It's apathetic. This guy clearly just wants to give up, go home and hand off his toga-toting deal-of-the-day onto the highest bidder.

It's not like Jon didn't do a thing the minute Will was set upon by lecherous harpies. He leapt to the defence too, ready to save his boss from lust and lipstick, judging by the look of intent on that vixen's face. He was just coming from a little further back, and Greg got in there first.

(And God. Will really, seriously, is not a damsel, or in distress. He isn't dressed for the role, for starters, okay? He would need some kind of mediaeval gown with a wimple and, and, a what do they have? A veil? Yeah, one of those. And a fool in motley, with bells. He can take care of *himself.*)

But Jon's come up by the stage, on the other side of Will to Greg, and is... not quite looking at Will. Staring away a little to the middle distance, breathing like he's controlling his temper – and Will didn't know that Jon had a temper, even.

Jon is too professional, at all times, to have a temper. Or at least to display it, on business premises, during working hours. Maybe not at a business-related social function, though. Possibly it doesn't count, or doesn't count enough, or he's just been pushed too far. Then he turns, and he turns to face Greg. Greg, who's already facing him by default, and perks up at the sniff of trouble, the eye-contact. This is ridiculous. But Will can't shake off the feeling of a couple of stray dogs eyeing each other, lost in a park and with a bone kicked between them, ripe for fighting over. Him?

There's an electric crackle in the dark dusty air of the function room, though, a vibe that could set thunderclouds on fire. It's perhaps a good thing that they're set either side of the auctioneer like bookends, far enough that... Well, beyond arms' reach, anyhow. And as if unconsciously picking up on the negative energy between them, the rest of the crowd has invisibly, undetectably, and yet clearly drawn back from the both of them a little bit. Who wants to get in the middle of a dog-fight? Not this bunch of nicely-brought-up genteel executive types, yeah that's for damn sure. They're at the two poles of a little pool of light and space and negative vibes, gazing at each other as Jon slams a hand down on the stage, and says three words – quite quietly, but it's still perfectly clear. That's how quiet the whole place suddenly is, breathless and hushed, waiting for a climax, for a resolution. "Eight-eighty, then."

And the auctioneer stares at him, visibly shrugs. And decides to go the whole hog, into full showman mode. "Eight hundred and eighty, people, do you hear that? Eight-eighty, for the pleasure and the privilege of this fine fella's company and service for the evening!" And here he leers repulsively at Will, who frowns back at him, more irritated than pissed-off. As *if,* is it likely? He may be on the wrong side of thirty, now – and he feels a little self-conscious over that, in relation to his feelings for Jon. Christ, an ancient asshole like him, fixating on a beautiful twenty-something, it has to be pretty pathetic, and if only Jon never realises it... "Cheap at the price!" the frilly-shirted shiny-tux'd asshole announces. "Who's going to go one better than that, my good people?"

"Nine hundred!" Greg yells. Just like his mom never taught him how to behave in public.

It's crazy. Crazy, a stupid amount of money, and Will has to hope, in spite of his true feelings on the matter, that Jon doesn't take the bait. If he did, then Will would surely have to reimburse him, because that's a ridiculous price, and Will can't expect him to come up with it out of his own salary just to make Will look good and help this damn stupid event be a success. And Will can't just lift it out of petty cash and expect the company to foot the bill, either. Petty cash! That would be unreasonable.

"Nine-fifteen," Jon says, but he says it slowly, like the actual amount he's pledging, for an extremely short-term and dubious good of limited utility, is finally coming home to him after a prolonged period of insanity. And the jump from nine hundred to nine hundred and fifteen bucks is smaller. Yeah, it's coming home to him exactly what he's doing, all right. But his mobile, sexy mouth is set in a line that won't budge, and he's looking stubborn as hell. And Will knows that look on Jon. He's seen it before, when a deal goes south, when a supplier's being an asshole. Jon takes a step towards Greg, like he's just daring him to make another bid. He doesn't flex his hands, doesn't ball them into fists. But Will can tell from the twitch of his hands, that he really, really wants to.

And hell with all this, because Will isn't letting this go any further. (He thinks wildly for a moment about jumping into the bidding himself, to win the prize of his own company and service for the evening. Except that he's pretty sure that the prize itself isn't supposed to be a part of the action. Plus he doesn't know exactly what kind of fun BDSM shenanigans he'd get up to, rewarded with his own company in a saucy toga, and some weighty and really amazingly uncomfortable chains.) But no, he wants something a bit more direct than that, a direct intervention to get immediate results. So he begins to move – to drag himself – the few steps to get closer to Jon, to get back in his eye-line. More accurately, to drag his ball and chains. God almighty, could they not have gone with plastic or foam rubber? Elizabeth, for God's sake!

It gets a cheer from the crowd. God, they're getting their money's worth tonight, a whole soap opera of entertainment, pursuit and romance, continuous drama. And he hisses at Jon, "What do you think you're doing? Just quit it. Leave it be, I'll talk to you tomorrow, I'll–"

And it does nothing, serves no purpose at all, because all it gets from Jon is a slow, sweet smile raised to Will's face. (His face is amused, a little bit. Well, how would he not laugh, considering the get-up that Will has been all but forced into, by three excitable and authoritative women with a vested interest in making money and rendering him a sex-object? He looks *ridiculous*.)

"Nine-fifty," Greg slurs in response, and he moves in a step himself, but not quite as steadily.

And Will can't tolerate this, can't accept it, because *nine-hundred-and-fifty dollars,* Christ almighty, everyone's lost their senses around here. And he doesn't give a damn just how good the cause is, they're all still basket-cases. He doesn't care, flings himself down on his knees to get face-to-face on the same level with Jon, eye to eye so the idiot can't avoid Will, can't refuse to engage and carry on in his own sweetly stubborn, charmingly oblivious way. The crowd absolutely love it – more drama, more! - and the whoops which are already a steady thrum of percussion, an intermittent irregular drumbeat, gather velocity and volume to become a swift pattering rainfall. (There are several suggestions about his toga and his body that Will is glad that he can't quite pick out of the general hum and hubbub.)

And no, Jon won't look at him, and it's not surprising as the next thing out of his mouth is a clear, cutting, "Nine hundred and seventy dollars!" The maniac. Will reaches out and grasps at his chin at that, because maybe that'll get his attention.

Which it does, because Jon doesn't resist. Instead he whips his head around immediately, looks fierce and unsmiling, wide brown eyes staring straight into

Will's. And in that moment he ducks his head and kisses Will, fast and sweet and surprising, pulling away and backing off suddenly. And if the crowd loved Will's rockabilly surge and glide to his knees, acrobatic and probably giving 'em more of a flash of his parts than he'd intended, then the whistles and catcalls at this point go *effing crazy*. Jon looks startled, flushed. It's pretty clear that none of that was pre-meditated. "Sorry," he says, fast and breathless.

At the same time as Greg, flushed and lush and handsome, heavyset and lurchingly unsteady on his feet now, also says, "Hey!" It's in a tone that strongly suggests that Jon's playing with *his* toys, and there's going to be a major discussion about that, because he ain't happy and he ain't having it, no. He looks from Jon, to Will, and back again, and back again. Maybe he's having a little trouble focusing. The glass of champagne in his hand wobbles a little bit. And maybe a few of the onlookers that the scene, as well as the auction, has attracted, are snickering a little, too. His mouth tightens up, and evidently he decides what it is that's going to fix this situation to his satisfaction. And he turns, heavy, definitely wobbling, to the auctioneer, catches his eye where it's wandering away like the guy would sooner be anywhere else, absolutely anywhere, sooner than here.

But there's a job to be done, God damn it! And Greg obviously thinks that he's the man to do it. Because he holds on tight to the rim of the stage, leans forward towards Jon and grins right in his face. That's as he yells out, easy loud enough to echo round the hall in the suddenly hushed silence, "Nine – hundred – and – ninety – nine – dollars! I bid!"

Yeah. The asshole. (The drunken asshole, to be fair. There's no guarantee that he's going to remember an action or a moment of this tomorrow, but right now? Right now, he's definitely a complete ass.)

It's the mark of an idiot and the work of an ass, and Will's mouth falls open, really in wonder at the sheer unashamed assholery of it, unrelieved, unleavened. Jon, on the other hand – he's red in the face and clearly furious. And he lifts shaking hands, like he's sorely tempted to just go ahead and shove a soddenly drunken man on his ass. If only it wouldn't make him just as much of an asshole as Greg.

Jon's tempted, but on the other hand Will is remorseless. (And he has no intention of being won for the night by Greg. Not *now*. Not after that kiss, no way. He puts out one fingertip towards Greg, where they're all three of them leaned in relatively close together, now. It's tempting. So tempting. One little push is all it would take.

Then, simultaneously... "Nine hundred and ninety-nine dollars I'm offered! Anyone care to improve upon that offer? Please God, someone improve upon that! I wanna put this baby to bed and go home to my baby!" the auctioneer pleads.

And also... A leering Greg takes one step closer, which puts him approximately toe-to-toe and nose-to-nose with a furiously-trembling Jon. Or it would – except he slips, where someone's spilled a little champagne on the floor, and he goes down on his ass, down on his ass, man, and it couldn't happen to a nicer guy, yeah, sure!

And in addition... Jon pulls a little away from Will (which is bad, a bad idea, wrong), looks away from him out into the crowd. And grins, white-smiled, white faced, a little wild-eyed. "A thousand bucks!" he yells.

It makes him crazy, officially crazy. And Will is crazy about *him*. And when he jumps up, onto the podium beside Will, and Greg is out cold on his ass with most of the drunken crowd paying very little attention, and the auctioneer is hammering away at his gavel and block and manically declaring, "Sold! Sold! Sold! To the crazy person with a thousand bucks in his pocket! Thank God, and I'm going home! Never again, you people are nuts!"... what can Will do but kiss Jon.

He definitely is going to pay him back, though. And it's worth every cent.

⟫—◉—⟪

AN HOUR LATER HIS EVENING is bought and paid for, his time hired out, in a dark corner of the ballroom associated with the charity function room the company's booked. And, obediently and according to strict instruction, he's holding still while Jon sits on his knee and pets his hair, squirming a little and getting it all disarranged and messy. "Do I really have to carry on wearing this stupid toga?" Will complains, and tries to put his hands up around Jon's waist, narrow and fine in his dress pants. "I've got a perfectly good suit back in my hotel room. Which we could be in right now, instead of in a dark dancehall where the booze has run out and the DJ has a 90s fixation. And the cake is wrecked." He can't move his hands far enough, anyway, and just has to suffer Jon's man-handling, instead. The rascal has used the chains Will is bound by to bind him further – wrapped them about his wrists and behind his back, so that he's effectively helpless. And Jon seems to like him that way.

Jon silences him with a kiss for a moment, which is acceptable. He nips along Will's top lip, little kisses and bites that make some high-pitched musical instrument hum and sing deep in Will's brain, make him a little dizzier than the three glasses he's had so far could possibly explain. Then rests his forehead against Will's, and says, "Behave yourself. I like the toga. You look good in it. More than good. You're fulfilling my every dirty fantasy. Or a few, anyway."

And his hands go behind Will's back, where his wrists are chained together, to linger and caress at the sore places where the chains are pulled tight, wrapped and wrapped again. "I'll set you free when I feel like it. You belong to *me*."

And this kiss is deeper, tongue searching into Will's mouth, so that he's shocked by the sweet giddy champagne-flavored kick of it. Oh, this is bold, this is very different from Jon's first hesitant approach when he claimed his purchase and led Will – clanking with chains like Marley's ghost – out of the auction room and across the hall. And he'd taken Will to the darkest corner of the ballroom/function room of the hotel, where the party was already beginning to break up and break down and dissipate, the balloons wilting, deflated, and the hectic hysterical party spirit dying on the vine.

Then, he'd been almost shy, evading Will's arms as Will pushed in eagerly for an embrace, eyes down in a thick fringe of lashes (and Jon never evades eye contact, never.) "Am I going to be fired, tomorrow?" he'd asked, and that had to be a joke, right?

So Will had laughed. "What for? What would I have you fired for?"

And Jon had looked about, at anything and anywhere but not at Will. "I don't know... sexual harrassment? Of my boss? Inappropriate behaviour at a work social function? Insanity?"

And somehow Will had pushed into the sweet hallowed space of his arms, looped a clanking chain about his neck to bring his lovely uncertain face closer. "Would it be worth it, if you were? Would it be *a thousand bucks* of *worth it*?"

Jon's face had relaxed at that, into glowingly happy and peaceful lines, and that was the correct reaction, the one that Will was after. "Absolutely," he'd said. "Worth every cent."

That kiss had been worth a thousand bucks, too. Easy.

But now, ten minutes later, Jon has recovered an awful lot of his usual level of confidence and outspoken self-assurance. You could call him cocky, even. He's maybe getting a little bit above himself. And the caress, as he brushes fingers over Will's cheek and smooths a hand through his disordered hair, is quite definitely proprietorial. "Sssssh," he says, dismissive. "We'll go when I tell you. I'm happy where I am, for the time being." And he rests his head on Will's shoulder, and gives a blissful sigh. "Do as you're told."

And Will feels a chuckle try to break free, tremble his chest where Jon's other hand rests upon it, warm and smugly possessive. "Should I?" he asks. "Are you the boss now? Are you the boss of *me*?"

"Better believe it," Jon agrees, warm and heavy on Will's lap, arms tight about him where he's helpless and bound, and perfectly happy. "Winning bid, remember? You're mine."

———◉———

THE END.